AMAZING CREATIONS

EDITED BY LYNSEY EVANS

First published in Great Britain in 2024 by:

Young Writers
Remus House
Coltsfoot Drive
Peterborough
PE2 9BF
Telephone: 01733 890066
Website: www.youngwriters.co.uk

Printed and bound in the UK by BookPrintingUK
Website: www.bookprintinguk.com
YB0587P

FOREWORD

For our latest competition, The Glitch, we asked secondary school students to turn the ordinary into the extraordinary by imagining an anomaly, something suddenly changing in the world, and writing a story about the consequences. Whether it's a cataclysmic twist of fate that affects the whole of humanity, or a personal change that affects just one life, the authors in this anthology have taken this idea and run with it, writing stories to entertain and inspire. We gave them an added challenge of writing it as a mini saga which forces them to really consider word choice and plot. We find constrained writing to be a fantastic tool for getting straight to the heart of a story.

The result is a thrilling and absorbing collection of tales written in a variety of styles, and it's a testament to the creativity of these young authors, and shows us just a fraction of what they are capable of.

Here at Young Writers it's our aim to inspire the next generation and instil in them a love of creative writing, and what better way than to see their work in print? The imagination and skill within these pages show that we might just be achieving that aim! Congratulations to each of these fantastic authors, they should be very proud of themselves.

CONTENTS

Alex Moore (16)	63
Ricky Friswell (16)	64
Lainey Milligan (16)	65
Haydn Inman (14)	66
Layton Mann (12)	67
Markus Burrell (15)	68
Tabitha Sayers (15)	69
Carys Homer (13)	70
Joshua Lumley (12)	71
Jamie Leigh (13)	72
Olivia Smart (16)	73
Peter Talbot (15)	74
Cian Orme (14)	75
Ethan Ames (15)	76
Alicia Sullivan (14)	77
Ana McClean (13)	78
Lexie Todd (15)	79
Charlie Hamilton (14)	80
Calum Wright (14)	81
Jake Greenway (17)	82
Mimi Currie (17)	83
Madeline Standley (15)	84
India Jackson (12)	85
Shaney-Ellis Fletcher (14)	86
Eve Wood (11)	87
Joshua Powis (15)	88
Bella Dowding (15)	89
Ashton Tomlinson (14)	90
Sophie Colley (13)	91
Joseph Williamson (17)	92
Lucas Smith (14)	93
Reid Howarth (12)	94
Jack Hollis (12)	95
Elliott Clarke (13)	96
Vanessa Wojcik (12)	97
Logan Madeley (12)	98
Alfie Southard (12)	99
Saely Gurung (15)	100
Noah Alfie Patey (17)	101
George Revell	102
Archie Parsons (13)	103
Baydon Moffat (12)	104
Ellsie Bagshaw (14)	105

Arlo Brown (15)	106
Oliver Lucking (14)	107
Annabel Soles (12)	108
Kitty Wearing (12)	109
Harry Mair Tilley (13)	110
Oliver Poole (13)	111

Sandbach School, Sandbach

Benjamin Head (13)	112
Brayden Fuller (14)	113
Joseph Broad (13)	114
Adam Machnik (14)	115
Evan Davies (13)	116
Jacob Baker (13)	117
Lucas Gibson (13)	118

THE
STORIES

THE LATE DEATH

Katy woke up, it was a dark gloomy day. A dark gloomy day turned into a confusing, worrying, terrifying day. She got out of bed and walked out of her room. Loud, calm music was playing and a lovely delicious smell entered her nose.

"Yum!" she shouted, walking into the kitchen.

"Argh!" Mum screamed. "Get out! Who are you?"

Katy was confused. "I'm Katy!" she said.

She then decided to phone her dad.

"Hello?"

"Dad, it's me, Katy," she said.

"Stop playing pranks, it's not funny."

"Huh?"

"Katy died two years ago..."

The call ended.

Heidi John (11)
All Saints CE Academy, Ingleby Barwick

WIPED OUT

'*Warning*, breaking news, the world is ending'.

"*What!*" exclaimed Mam.

'We have some more intel. Five minutes until the asteroid hits'.

Sprinting out of the house, no time for belongings.

"Come on, hurry up! Get in," exclaimed Mam. "Oh no! There is loads of traffic. Quick, get out."

Sprinting for our lives, Daisy led the way to the shuttle. At the site there were loads of people at the gates, looks of rage on their faces.

"Aww, so sorry, the shuttle is full," exclaimed the pilot with a cheap smug look on her face.

Too late. *Bang!* Humanity's lost.

Lucy Bowler (11)

All Saints CE Academy, Ingleby Barwick

THE END

He woke up again and went to work... again. Driving through the empty roads, his mind in knots, he arrived at 'work'. Now endless rows of fields.

"W-what?" he stuttered.

Thump, thump, thump. His heart raced as if it wanted to leap out of his body. Confusion slowly absorbed his whole mind. A scream echoed from afar. Fast footsteps went from ear to ear.

"Hello," he screeched.

A tall skinny figure crept abnormally towards him.

"Well, hello," the unknown figure replied in a rattling voice. Hallucinating codes, breathing fast, heart pumping. Blank... his mind went blank. Was this the end?

Freya Hicks (11)
All Saints CE Academy, Ingleby Barwick

THE REFLECTION

I woke up and headed to the bathroom to check on my hair. I looked in the mirror and screamed, "My reflection... it's moving!"

Its beady eyes stared into my soul. My eyes were looking in horror, my heart was beating as fast as light. I heard my mum coming.

"Lucy! Are you alright? I heard a scream."

Silence fell in the house. The person in the mirror looked at the door and spoke, "See you tomorrow," with a beady smile.

"Lucy, talk to me!" my mum shouted.

"I-I-I"

I fainted and everything went black like the world had disappeared...

Aimee Roberts (12)
All Saints CE Academy, Ingleby Barwick

MORTE BONJOUR

A hotel bygone, distinguished by the deathly aura that surrounds it; its name is Morte Bonjour, but it's abandoned. A company, Coperx, builds an underground lab, but also, a dangerous experiment goes disastrously wrong. A pressure bar goes loose, and the air turns toxic, killing every living organism in sight.

A school of children were playing inside the Morte Bonjour, and the toxic fumes entered the lungs of the little group, but one held his and watched in horror as his friends melted into figures beyond explanation. He let out an ear-piercing scream, which resulted in him becoming a misshapen figure.

Leonard Udeagha (12)
All Saints CE Academy, Ingleby Barwick

THE GLITCH IN TIME

Mesmerised, I stared at the elaborate paintings on the walls of Menkaure's burial chamber. But something wasn't right. They moved. Images seemed to dance off the walls in an expansive array of colours. Powerful gods turned and smiled. Well, as much as they could with the head of a jackal. Before long, I was surrounded by people... from the paintings! They escorted me outside, my hoody now the finest silk, and I was adorned with golden jewellery. Waves of people bowed to me.

"All hail the Pharaoh of Egypt!"

I froze.

"There must be a glitch here somewhere," I muttered.

Beth Fowle (15)
All Saints CE Academy, Ingleby Barwick

GLITCHING

Where am I? What's happening to me? Suddenly, it hit him. He was travelling through space and time.

Ralph recalls his memory, remembering he found a mysterious door and behind the door was a wall, but glitching. It sucked him in and led him to this. This endless abyss. Ralph finally woke up, wondering where he was. Suddenly, a dragon flew by, a glitching dragon flashing colours of all kinds.

"There's a dragon, there's a dragon, help me!" shouted Ralph.

Instincts kicked in suddenly and an impressive jet of water came out of Ralph's hand, somehow killing the dragon. But how?

Guan Chen Ding (11)
All Saints CE Academy, Ingleby Barwick

CORRUPTED

"You're early," said Death.

I exited my homely shack-house, scouring for berries for a new antidote against the corrupted. Five years ago, the AI took over. I turned the corner and there they were. They tailed me, but I thought nothing of it because I believed they were my fellow comrades until they weren't. It was too late. I ran to the top of the Empire State Building, my blood boiling. I was terrified. I couldn't become one of them, and I wouldn't. So I jumped. My comrades... at least they were safe now.

"You're early," said Death.

Finally freedom...

Evie Halasz (12)
All Saints CE Academy, Ingleby Barwick

THE GLITCH

Ignoring the warnings, Franky downloaded the app. Every clock stopped. The whole world froze. Little did Franky know that he'd just released a dangerous virus. The virus started to spread, colours flashed, screens cracked, the virus hacked every computer system as it made its way through the city. The world was still frozen, and time still stopped. Every phone, computer, TV and electronic device shut down, completely destroyed. Imagine a world without devices; well, that was what Franky was thinking at that very moment. *What have I done? Will my world ever be the same again...?*

Daniel Leighton (12)
All Saints CE Academy, Ingleby Barwick

THE TIME STOPPER

"For the record, Sergeant Barnes. To stop every major war, we have created the Time Stopper."
Little did he know this would destroy every civilisation.
"The Time Stopper has been lost, yet the tracker says it's in my house. No, it-it can't be..."
As Barnes rushed home, time stopped. *I've got to get home*, thought Barnes, irritated.
When he got home, he went to his son, Jeremy, who said, "Hi Daddy, you're early. Cool watch!"
"Can I have it back, Jeremy?"
"Yes, just let me press this..."

Luke Nevison (11)
All Saints CE Academy, Ingleby Barwick

THE GLITCH

Ignoring the warnings, I downloaded the app. Suddenly, my king-sized bed disappeared, my phone screen seemed to crack and split and everything around me vanished like a ghost. Colours of orange, blue and purple, swirled around me, making me feel like I was in a tornado. *Plop.* And there I stood, on the spot, in a dimension that looked like... No, it couldn't be. Like my comics on the multiverse. Looking around I noticed that it looked like the multiverse from Doctor Strange's movie. Heart beating, mind all confuzzled, I knew what I had to do. I had to finish the game.

Maryam Kagzi (12)
All Saints CE Academy, Ingleby Barwick

THE GRIM REAPER GLITCH

Pat woke up with a huge smile on his face, it was the last day of school. He got ready and off he went. When he entered the gates his head glitched off his body. Then, he found himself standing on clouds in a queue. Once he was at the front...

"Next! You're early," said Death. "What happened?"

"Where am I?" replied Pat.

"You're not supposed to be here are you?" said the Grim Reaper.

And with a flash, he was sat next to Katrina Donelly listening to Mr Browning talking about the formation of rocks. What just happened?

Connor Campbell (11)

All Saints CE Academy, Ingleby Barwick

WONDERS OF THE WORLD (GLITCH)

Somehow, her reflection was moving, but the thing was, she wasn't! How was this possible? It was surely a dream, so she blinked and carried on getting ready. She was walking to school.

"Hey Skylar," someone exclaimed. It was her friends, but she saw the reflection again, but it was a shadow this time.

"What do you want?" and it wandered off.

It followed her everywhere; to school, in class, on the toilet! What did it want from her? It still followed her home. When she looked in the mirror it pulled her arm in. It was another universe!

Megan Simmons (12)
All Saints CE Academy, Ingleby Barwick

THE CELESTIAL WAR

Creatures armed to the teeth slowly lumbered across the battlefield, over the scorching bodies. I turned to my friend. "We should not have come here!" Jack said.

"Well, if we have to, we will put up a good fight," I said as an energy blade formed in my hand.

"Okay, if you say so..." said Jack, uncertainly, forming a red-hot fireball in his hands.

I looked at him, smiled, and said, "Just don't get killed and we'll win. Okay?"

"Got it!" said Jack as we faced the incoming horde of aliens...

Dexter Wright (12)
All Saints CE Academy, Ingleby Barwick

LAST SURVIVOR

The sun hadn't risen for ten years, the world had stopped, all of it. Except one boy.

The sky was covered in UFOs. He woke up and called for his mum. No response. He called again. No response. Quickly, he got up from his bed and looked at his phone. The 24th of August 2673. "What?" he asked himself.

His parents and sister weren't in their bedroom. Slowly, he walked up to the window in his living room.

They saw him. The aliens were all looking at him. His eyes widened. "Why are they looking at me?" That was it. The chase began.

Pippa Argument (11)
All Saints CE Academy, Ingleby Barwick

THE DARK SUN

In the year 3023, the sun never rose. Frantically, scientists and experts tried to work out the problem. They sent rockets and tried to see what was going on through satellites, but they would never work. Riley, an 11-year-old girl filled with curiosity, wanted to find the cause of this as she was living in misery. Bravely, she left her house but got sucked up in an extremely powerful ray. Darkness. When she awoke she saw them. Something she'd never imagined she'd see. Aliens. But something was off about them. Then they took off their masks, they were humans!

Aiza Shahid (12)
All Saints CE Academy, Ingleby Barwick

THE GIRL WHO FROZE TIME

The world was changing, people were changing. The game. Fighting for their lives. What if they all died? The game began. "Go!" They shoot.

Some dying, more hiding. Some were greedy, some experienced, some not. The clock stopped. Everyone stopped in time, except a small girl.

Frightened, she shot the girl next to her, not realising it was her sister. The clock started ticking. The players unfroze and shoot each other again.

They all died, except the girl who stopped the game before she collapsed and all died. *Bang!* The owner won.

Layla Cattle (12)
All Saints CE Academy, Ingleby Barwick

THE LOST CHILD

I woke up as my dog started to growl.

"Benjamin?" I asked. "Come here, what's wrong?"

He leapt and scratched the wall. I stood there confused and then told him to leave because I was going to get changed. I closed the door and went to the bathroom. I jumped. I was sure I had seen something more in the mirror.

Back in the bedroom, I shivered all of a sudden. *Bang!* Lights went off. Silence. I heard a cry from the wall.

"Benjamin?"

He was gone! It laughed, every night doing the same thing until...

Gracie Dixon (11)
All Saints CE Academy, Ingleby Barwick

THE DEVIL'S DRAWING

Mae looked under her daughter's bed as she was doing her room. She grabbed a piece of paper that was stored under the small gap beneath the bed and inspected it. Fleur's drawing wasn't happy like usual. It had a drawing of her mum, Mae, surrounded by black-horned, red, devil-like creatures. Mae felt a shiver run down her spine as she realised this was the future. Her jaw agape and her eyes wide, her hands trembling and loosening their grip on the paper, the sheet fell onto the floor as Mae stood up, her mind running a million miles per second.

Haveen Affan (11)
All Saints CE Academy, Ingleby Barwick

THE WAR BEGINNING

Just a normal Monday at Redcliffe High School. 9am, first lesson back after the long summer. Joe had a long, hard lesson in maths, and went to English for an hour, which didn't turn out the way he wanted it to have. Then the only lesson Joe didn't like was history and that was third. He reluctantly got out of his seat to go then, *bang!* The screaming, the shouting, the fleeing. Then the soldiers came. The air raid siren went off and he was lucky to have escaped. Soldiers were taking teachers off to start training for the war.

Bobby Caswell (12)
All Saints CE Academy, Ingleby Barwick

UNTITLED

Ignoring the warnings from her parents, Ava downloaded the app. All of her friends had downloaded this app so she thought she would be fine, but little did she know what was going to happen next. Ava's face rapidly changed.

This mysterious app said that she had five minutes left. Ava was petrified to see this, she threw her phone across the room. Ava nervously waited as five minutes passed by. Suddenly her screen began to split, it was almost like a black hole opened in her phone. She felt a strong force pulling her in. Ava was trapped.

Hollie Parrish (11)
All Saints CE Academy, Ingleby Barwick

HOW THE GRINCH LIKED CHRISTMAS

The Grinch had the best idea yet, to steal Christmas on Christmas Eve. He went around all the houses and stole Christmas but, suddenly, he was standing outside a pet shop and Max was in there. He was just a puppy, it looked like the Grinch teleported back years. Someone came and bought Max on Christmas Day. He was happy with his family at Christmas but they got a cat and had to put him down. Now Max was sad at Christmas because he never celebrated, so the Grinch gives all the presents back and celebrates Christmas with Max, and is the best.

Isabel Parker (11)
All Saints CE Academy, Ingleby Barwick

FORGOTTEN

Once upon a Saturday evening, a beautiful family had a baby girl and named her Harriet. She was a very playful girl. Twelve years passed, and Harriet turned into a pretty, charming young teenager.

One stormy night, Harriet was walking home, she opened the door but there was a mysterious-looking lady. She looked pale and she had a black cloak. She peeked through the door and saw her mum working for her. She called out to her mum but she just ran up and smacked her head and made her unconscious. Her mum didn't even know who she was.

Gurjapji Kaur (12)
All Saints CE Academy, Ingleby Barwick

CAN'T BREATHE

Repeating the movements, over, under, over, under. The pool was empty and I decided to challenge myself to breathe at the bottom of the pool. Bravely, I swam to the bottom and spotted a glowing purple portal. Curiously, I swam through the portal and suddenly whizzed through a big slide and landed in the bottom of the ocean. Panicking, I searched for air because I couldn't breathe. A glow of air looked so far away and I tried to reach it. Minutes later, I still couldn't reach it, until a dark figure swam toward me. A shark!

Hana-May Ghafoor (11)
All Saints CE Academy, Ingleby Barwick

THE MUSIC BOX

As I awakened, I could sense a strange, unnatural feeling. However, I discovered an antique box... A record player? I found it weird. I could hear my mother in the kitchen so I decided to play it. Then the sizzling sound of bacon stopped. Creeping into the kitchen, I found my mother frozen in place. I gasped at the sight of all of this. Quickly, I sprinted outside. This was no joke. I went out to scream, but I caught a glimpse of movement. If I saw it I thought it must've seen me. Standing still, it glared straight at me...

Isla Richardson (11)
All Saints CE Academy, Ingleby Barwick

MOTIONLESS

Every clock stopped, we were stuck in a time loop and only I could stop it. Cautiously, I crept outside when suddenly... I saw a flash of light so bright my eyes almost blinded! Before my eyes stood a girl with her little dog motionless! Hypnotisted even. A bird was frozen in mid-flight, almost like it was paused. Some time passed. I continued investigating until I figured out that the only living thing was me, but how? No movement, no help, just me.

Tap, tap. A knock on the door. *I'm not the only one!*

Priya Jethwa (12)
All Saints CE Academy, Ingleby Barwick

RISEN

The sun hasn't risen for five years. Our world is dying. People are fighting. The streets are dangerous. This hasn't changed. This is the day our world changed. Nine thousand died in the first five months. People died from lack of food and hydration. Some were killed in a fight. Animals were desperate, eating whatever they possibly could. The borders where dark and light met were where they fought for food. Some people camped there, but they didn't make it through the night. Our world will soon be gone.

Scarlett Smith (11)

All Saints CE Academy, Ingleby Barwick

MY UFO

Life was quiet. Like really quiet. Quieter than the time I found out Aunt Lucy had died. Something wasn't right. Suddenly, there was a colossal bang. I looked out the window and there it was. Something we'd all seen in books and fiction but we'd never properly seen before. None of us. A UFO. It glided along the sky like a cloud. Its lights blinded people from miles away. Life felt, well, it didn't really feel like anything, actually. All of a sudden, I felt a slimy, scaly hand crawl up my back...

Poppy Short (12)
All Saints CE Academy, Ingleby Barwick

MYSTERIOUS MIRRORS

James was a normal kid with normal clothing and a normal life. One day, at his school, he was learning about mirrors. He glanced at one, he was completely motionless, but his reflection wasn't. He closed his eyes slowly and then opened them again. He thought he was in a dream. He didn't know what to do!

Then it talked. "James!" it said.

Then he realised, his face looked a bit odd. Then he noticed that when he moved his head, it stayed the same. Now he knew, it was his twin behind the glass.

Adam Harkin (11)
All Saints CE Academy, Ingleby Barwick

DOWN

I gagged in the seabed. I was being pushed down. Icy water pierced my skin. Down, down, down... I gasped for air, coughing. Suddenly, time stopped. Just stopped. I rushed up the water, bloody cuts dripping. I stood up shivering, crying. A dark figure came walking up to me.
"Who are you? Tell me now! Who are you?"
"No."
The shadow gently flicked my forehead. Down. I plunged down below. No one was there but I felt it, I heard it. It stung, but I knew. I was falling down...

Alvina Nahian (12)
All Saints CE Academy, Ingleby Barwick

THE HAUNTED HOUSE

He opened the door. *Screech!* Then he stepped into the old mansion. Anxiously, he walked into the living room, it was all destroyed wood with holes in the ceiling. It was a mess. The boy left the room, scared of what was coming next.
He went up the stairs into the bedroom. The toilet in the room was full of spiders and worms and webs from the spiders. The bed was mouldy and disgusting. It made him feel sick, so he left. He walked to the next room and opened the door.
"Argh!"

Luca Carlin (11)
All Saints CE Academy, Ingleby Barwick

THE NIGHT WITH THE FULL MOON...

It began on a night with a full moon. I glanced at the window. It was like the moon was telling me to follow it. All of a sudden, I was outside. It led to a dark, gloomy forest. Leaves rustled. I peered over the lake. I couldn't believe my eyes when I saw the reflection. A werewolf. Ears appeared. Fangs appeared. It was like the bright white moon controlled me. I opened my mouth.
Howl! Howl! Howl!
I kept howling until...

Millie Small (12)
All Saints CE Academy, Ingleby Barwick

TINKERBELL

I woke with a bang. I felt weird... like I had shrunk.
Clambering out of my bed, I dawdled to my large mirror.
Where was I? Where had I gone?
"Peter, is that you?"
"Yes, who is this?"
"Me, Tinkerbell."
"No... no... she died last year."
"What? No, I'm standing right in front of you!"
"No, she's dead!"
"Am I actually dead?"

Poppy Bacon (12)
All Saints CE Academy, Ingleby Barwick

APOCALYPSE

Silence was lurking and it was lurking good. Everywhere was silent, as I couldn't hear the *tick-tock* of the clock. I went to the town square and couldn't believe my eyes. A plane was in mid-air, suspended in motion, and I saw time. Time had stopped, everyone had stopped, aside from me... Then I saw chaos. I saw an eye erupt from the ground. It was the apocalypse. It had begun...

Dave Toni-Falade (12)
All Saints CE Academy, Ingleby Barwick

THE NEVER-ENDING TIMER

Millions gathered to watch. My eyes were fixed on the never-ending timer. Or so we thought. The more I looked at it, it seemed to be going faster. Five... four... three... Time was running out. Two... one... zero... I braced myself but when I opened my eyes, I wasn't in my own body. Just someone in a lonely coffee shop. In the corner of my eye, black flashes consumed everything but me...

Evie Richardson (12)
All Saints CE Academy, Ingleby Barwick

THE BOY WHO SHOULDN'T HAVE GROWN

"What is happening?" I said.

"You are growing, Peter," Tinkerbell said.

I didn't know what was happening. This is not supposed to happen! We were shocked!

"You have grown into a man, Peter," explained Tinkerbell.

"Your legs are going to keep growing!"

Tinkerbell was right because the growth never ever stopped.

Elana Harston (11)
All Saints CE Academy, Ingleby Barwick

THE DOMINO EFFECT

It all started on that fateful evening, I was in the living room of my house when I noticed something strange. I looked around and saw nothing but this cloud of smoke was coming towards me.
I ran and ran and ran, not understanding why this was happening until it hit me... me! I caused it! The darkness was the smoke which came from the power plant which came from me!

Casey Roberts (12)
All Saints CE Academy, Ingleby Barwick

THE HAUNTED HOUSE

It was a dark, deep and gloomy, Thursday night. Everything was normal until a large mysterious house caught my eye. I had to go in.

There was a broken clock hanging off the wall which was weird enough but then I realised the time was 2:50, the exact time I was born. Then a wooden plank started collapsing from the roof, missing my shoulders by an inch...

Seb Todd (12)
All Saints CE Academy, Ingleby Barwick

FROZEN IN TIME

Every clock had stopped. As she went to the kitchen, she heard no noise. Normally, she heard the clock all the time, ringing in her ear. Everyone was as still as a statue, not moving. She had no idea what was happening. The whole world had frozen, except for her. Then, suddenly, she heard a noise. *Tick-tock*, rang the clock.

Sophie Piggott (11)
All Saints CE Academy, Ingleby Barwick

WHAT IF ROBOTS WON?

What if robots developed a mind of their own? People were hiding, if you rebelled you died.
One day, I went out to get lunch and when I came back there was blood everywhere. My mum, dad, dog and sister were all on the floor dead. I knew what I had to do. I had to rebel...

Amelia Garbutt (11)
All Saints CE Academy, Ingleby Barwick

THE GLITCH

Every clock stopped... except for a subtle glitch sound.
Suddenly, an eight-legged spider with a clock on its
forehead leapt, missing me by millimetres. My heart raced
until I realised the beast was trapped behind the screen of
the iPad I was holding.
Once, twice, thrice. The spider couldn't escape the iPad.
After one last try, the screen cracked and the violent
creature took one strike. It gashed my face.
What was happening? My hands. My face. Pixelated. I was
pixelated now. Permanently. I couldn't speak or move.
The last thing I saw was the spider emerging from my room.

Benedict O'Flinn (11)
Epsom College, Epsom

THE RISE

Tom looked up; the resplendent city was silent and serene. The voluminous accommodations were glittering like thousands of stars painted across the stygian sky. Then it happened. People besieged the streets, flabbergasted, and yet the sun didn't rise. After a while, the once pure city turned abysmal. Carnage filled the air as belligerent people battled, the once ostentatious land turned barren and corrupt. Five years later; the ancient city was now deserted and abandoned, and only one human was left. He wandered around the city and then saw it; a cryptic beam of light shone down and the sun rose.

Liam Singh (11)
Epsom College, Epsom

THE GLITCH

Faint screams were coming from the back rooms, and the lights were flickering uncontrollably. The ostentatious chandeliers were swinging and shattering onto me slowly. The clocks were swift, moving faster than ever. Suddenly, everything stopped; the clocks, screams, lights, chandeliers, everything. I was trapped in the eerie darkness, but it seemed that I was disappearing. I couldn't feel myself, and it was extremely mystifying. Slowly my eyes opened. I was in a small room, consisting of only a bed, which I seemed to be lying on. There weren't any windows or doors. How was I going to escape?

Philippa Lackenby (12)
Epsom College, Epsom

REPETITION

I found money on the ground. I picked it up and a millisecond later, a bolt of lightning pounded my spine and my life stopped. Scenes of my life were rolling through in front of me rapidly. Blackness.

Suddenly, I awoke and everything was different. Everybody looked extremely dangerous and there wasn't a single colour to strike the eye. I walked around and saw something familiar. It was the same £10 note that I'd seen about ten minutes before.

I decided to pick it up. A bolt of lightning hit me straight after. Scenes of my life were rolling through in front of me. Blackness.

Charles Mackrell (11)
Epsom College, Epsom

THE GLITCH

I was wrong about him; he could be trusted. It's too late now.
It all started when he ran out of the asylum, that weird boy who looked exactly like me. He said he was from the future and if I didn't save him we'd all perish but I ignored him. Later, I saw him on the news - 'food poisoning' - and it was just the day after when half the population died; then half of that, then half again until only eight of us remained. Soon, they discovered that microscopic creatures were killing us from the inside. That's when they all dropped dead.

Gregory Parnaby (11)
Epsom College, Epsom

UNTITLED

There I was. In front of me were strange-looking forms, all sprawled out on a desk. Slowly, I reached out. One delicious second later, my body started to glitch, building up unsettling mist around me.

Crash!

I looked around. *Where am I?* I thought.

Time had passed since I was there and I had barely been able to move. I was probably going to die of starvation.

Is there really no food on this planet? I thought to myself. Suddenly, someone tapped me on the back.

"I've been watching you!"

Bailie Mackintosh (11)

Epsom College, Epsom

MALFUNCTION?

Ignoring the warnings, I downloaded the app. Then suddenly it felt like everything froze. I could not move a muscle. I was scared. I called for help but no one heard. Suddenly, everything went black, then I opened my eyes. It was a digital world. There were humans, but they were half-robot. This humungous one said, "Follow me."
I followed him into a room. He said, "Welcome to the computer."
I was stuck, but suddenly I closed my eyes and I was home. I was not sure what had happened. Was it a dream, or was it real?

Felix Kapsalis (11)
Epsom College, Epsom

OBSIDIAN CITY

The world had been perfect, but then there was a glitch in the system. People disappeared. Flames entered my room and I pushed against the door. It opened and I jumped down the stairs and into the street. It was them. A surreal fog filled what looked like a body. They were shooting the street with flame throwers. Blue fire surrounded me and made me choke. I pulled out my shotgun and aimed, fired, killing four, but a body fell on me. The audience cheered. The stage light hit my eyes.

"Ladies and gentlemen, the winner of the Glitch!"

Imogen Scott (12)
Epsom College, Epsom

GLITCHES

I was in the middle of a research project and saw a compelling-looking tab on my computer screen: 'accept' or 'retry'. I clicked 'accept', unaware of what was going to happen. Everything suddenly came to a halt. My screen, the ticking clock, the cold-sounding screeches of the crows outside, the falling drops of rain and snow drifting down lighter than a feather. I was completely mind-blown. What had happened? Was I dead? Was I okay? What should I do? My mind was racing with thoughts so much that I passed out.

Ted Macmillan (11)
Epsom College, Epsom

THE START OF THE END

Every clock had stopped. The resplendent city of London fell asleep. The mechanical gasps of trains paused under a wave of colour that reached across the vast city. The voluminous buildings peered down at me through the old tree, whose fingers stretched out across my lit-up face. It only occurred to me how abysmal this was after I took it all in. My lungs started choking on ash. My head was swimming. My heart was pounding on my rib cage. My arms felt like enervated sticks being trampled on. I gasped for air but nothing came out.

Oliver Lopez-Jones (12)
Epsom College, Epsom

THE EERIE SILENCE

The town went silent. All the clocks had stopped. The entire village suddenly fell into an eerie silence. Someone had put an end to the endless ticking of the clocks. It was pitch-black and Jimmy woke up to the sound of helicopter blades cutting through the air. Shortly after, Jimmy was climbing up the cold stone wall of Big Ben. Upon reaching the top, he saw a faint shadow, silhouetted against a far wall, but as soon as he saw it, it was gone. He couldn't make out what it was and went to investigate, but it had vanished.

Lauren Lees (12)
Epsom College, Epsom

THE GLITCH

As soon as I clicked, I knew it was a mistake. I should never have let that stranger into my computer. Now that stupid rascal can access all my personal data.

This is terrifying. How am I going to explain this to my parents? Will I need to leave home? I can feel my heart thumping inside me. My mouth is drying up. My belly feels like it's full of butterflies. I know in minutes my account will be drained and all personal information leaked.

It's too late to call my bank and plead for my money. It's over.

Will Ratcliffe (12)
Epsom College, Epsom

THE REMOTE

On Thursday I was watching my favourite episode of 'Friends', snuggled up into my blanket all warm. I took the remote and pressed the fast-forward button and all of a sudden I felt queasy.

I looked at the remote and it was disappearing, the living room was disappearing to pitch-blackness. Where was I? What was I doing here? My body was now a glowing outline. I wanted someone to comfort me.

With dozens of bright flashes in my eyes, I finally came back to real life. It must have been a glitch.

Alessandra Mansour (11)
Epsom College, Epsom

THE REFLECTION

Once, a girl was looking in the mirror when all of a sudden, a figure moved across the back of the reflection. She thought nothing, it was probably just a hallucination. But as the same figure kept on appearing, the girl got scared, as if it was real and somebody was somehow in her room. But one day, when she looked in the mirror, it wasn't just a shaded figure, it was a face, one not of a human. Terrified, she screamed, but as soon as she let out a noise, her reflection was gone and then so was she.

Mimi Peer (12)
Epsom College, Epsom

THE SUBMARINE

"Picking up movement ahead," the radio crackled into my ear as I kept the submarine forward.

"I've got no life signatures. Nothing on the radar either," I replied, unable to see anything, "maybe a malfunction?"

"Rog', recalibrating sensors."

There was a minute of silence before I got a follow-up.

"Nope, still picking it up."

"We're one of the first to explore Titan's depths, the cold's probably screwing with it. How close does it read?"

"Movement's erratic. I can't-"

The sub rattled, metal groaning.

"Right... switching to sonar, hopefully-"

Something slammed against the sub, smashing it into a cliff. Power lost, escape impossible.

Fin Shaw (15)
Exhall Grange School, Ash Green

AN UNLIKELY ALLIANCE

"You're early," said Death curiously, "what happened?"
Life dropped to her knees, her amber eyes begging for
salvation. Tears were threatening to stream down her face,
her façade smashing to pieces like a porcelain doll.
"You can't possibly let them die," she whimpered
persuasively, "we absolutely must save them. They have
something to live for."
Death was about to roll his eyes until he saw the
picturesque house engulfed in flames. Ungodly screams
were heard as the children desperately tried to escape their
fate. Unless...
Death reached for Life's hand, squeezing it reassuringly.
"Just this once."
Life smiled blissfully. "Deal."

Lucy Rees (16)
Exhall Grange School, Ash Green

THE HOTEL

Suddenly, I was teleported into what looked like a hotel of some sort. However, something didn't seem right. I grabbed the key to door one and opened it, but there were more. I went through doors two, three, four, five, six, seven, eight, nine, ten, eleven, twelve, thirteen, and fourteen, but at fifteen, the lights flickered and ominous sounds echoed all around.

I heard a creature groaning. I'd already gone through door sixteen, and there was nowhere to hide. Then, a grey-looking ball lunged at me, and then... silence. I was to stay there endlessly. I could check out of this hotel, but I could never leave. I was doomed.

Rowan Conroy (13)
Exhall Grange School, Ash Green

THE GLITCH

I was relaxing in my house watching some TV. The television went off and wouldn't switch on again. I put two new batteries in the remote but nothing happened. I checked downstairs but nothing was moving. I thought, *why has everything stopped?* At that moment I knew time had stopped. I went outside but nothing was moving. I thought, *am I dreaming?*

Behind me, an unknown entity whispered, "No."

I said, "Why are you here?"

"Time has stopped, the world needs to rest," he muttered.

I found myself frozen in an endless void for the rest of time. Help me.

Roman Lawrence-Chamberlain (13)
Exhall Grange School, Ash Green

UNTITLED

Jeremiah was startled and confused when Death appeared before him, claiming he was early and asking what had happened.

"I don't know," Jeremiah replied. "One minute I was walking along the crowded street, then I heard aggressive shouting, screaming and a very loud gunshot. The next thing I knew, I was transported here, to this dark and foreboding place," he explained.

Death gave him the very welcome news that he could return, but his life expectancy would be halved. Jeremiah paused for a while to consider his two options and eventually agreed. Death returned him instantly to his world.

Jago Potter (13)
Exhall Grange School, Ash Green

THE PRICE OF LOVE

Two star-crossed lovers from warring planets fell in love on a peace-seeking mission that went disastrously wrong. They secretly met each other even though their respective governments were enemies. They were forced to choose between their lives or to prove that peace could be reached by exposing their relationship to the world. They risked losing everything, including their lives and the planets. If their presidents found out they would be murdered, but they had to protect their families secret. They needed to take control no matter what the consequences were. They knew they would be traitors to protect world peace.

Grace Wheeler (15)
Exhall Grange School, Ash Green

ALIEN

Unexpectedly, I woke up around 12am. A massive object flew past my window. *Boom!* Something hit the floor! A mystery shape lay flat on the ground. On closer inspection, its windows were massive circles which glowed and shimmered on the outer metal shell. *Beep, beep, beep* automatic stairs descended to the ground. Footsteps could be heard tapping against the metal. Unexpectedly, I had come face-to-face with an indescribable creature. It was tall and green. Its black eyes were like black holes. I wanted to scream but the sound I made was just a croak.
"What are you?" I squeaked.

Chloe-Leigh Wesson (12)
Exhall Grange School, Ash Green

CONFRONTED BY THE PAST

Entering the laboratory there are mirrors everywhere. An eerie voice calls out my name. I hold my ears tightly; hoping the voices will stop. Without warning, blood rains down on me!

Slowly the voice creeps into my mind absorbing my thoughts. They are now playing like a movie on a million screens. I'm surrounded. The clock ticks, *tick-tock...* Time is running out!

The clock strikes 12:00. All the mirrors smash into pieces. The voices disappear; my past confronts me. Out of the shadows, a door beams a blinding light into my eyes. A voice shouts, "Fight these negative demons!"

Mollie Clarke (17)

Exhall Grange School, Ash Green

THE SUN HADN'T RISEN FOR FIVE YEARS

The sun hadn't risen for five years.

One day, without warning, the sun suddenly glowed brightly in the sky and kept shining. It was like being woken up from the dead. Perhaps the environmental catastrophe scientists warned us about was over?

The solar panels on the rooftops were functioning again. The birds suddenly awoke, flowers started to bloom and the breeze was warm and balmy. Under a bright blue sky, people were happy, relaxed and contented for a while. The world had come back to life.

Two months later, the world exploded as temperatures soared. All life had ended as predicted.

Alex Moore (16)
Exhall Grange School, Ash Green

EVERY CLOCK HAD STOPPED...

It is 2199.
A black-clothed man called Ricky flew across a crowded, fluorescent city with buildings so packed together there was almost no spare ground. The car flew across the mirage of tall towers. Suddenly, every clock had stopped. The flying car froze like a musical statue. Ricky bumped himself. He ended up with broken bones and couldn't have treatment. Ricky thought it couldn't get any worse. It didn't take out his joyfulness though. Ricky slowly started to crawl down the ten thousand-foot tower with unimaginable nervousness, like a tarantula. Ricky then jumped to hallowed ground.

Ricky Friswell (16)
Exhall Grange School, Ash Green

NEW YORK SECRET REVEALED

Flight 59 to New York. On board was John Miller, a business manager and Claire Milligan, who, bored by her marriage, was looking for a richer, more attractive husband. They met on the flight and had an affair while in New York. Their partners were oblivious. A week later they returned on Flight 59. They both said goodbye and headed to the arrivals lounge to meet their respective partners, separately. Their secret would never be revealed, or so they thought. The front page news headline and photograph on every newspaper that day: 'British couple enjoy unprecedented temperatures in Central Park'.

Lainey Milligan (16)
Exhall Grange School, Ash Green

DEATH'S CONFUSION

I am alone with no one to accompany me, except Death. His pearly white skeleton contrasts with his deep black robe. His eyes are a gaping hole in his skull, which continuously gleam at you.

"What happened?" said Death, the holes in his skull widened to assert his interest. I didn't respond. "You weren't meant to die," said Death. His face was perplexed, installing fear into me, as Death did not know. "I must go," said Death, his voice now had a small tremor. He dissolved into a pile of ash and disappeared. My hands trembled as I awaited Death's order.

Haydn Inman (14)
Exhall Grange School, Ash Green

SUPPORT NEEDED URGENTLY

My name is Zacha Farrag. I wake up, dress, eat breakfast... the usual mundane routine. Opening my door, I am surprised to find it is locked. Turning around, I am frozen to the spot, my room is upside down. I look through my window; there is nothing but darkness. The room starts spinning, ornaments, lights and books fly about in all directions. It's like being in a tumble dryer. I manage to open the window. I fall through the window. The world has suffered a terrible glitch. I am in the void.

"Help!" I scream hysterically. "Support requested. Support needed urgently!"

Layton Mann (12)
Exhall Grange School, Ash Green

YoungWriters® Est. 1991

EVERY FORTNIGHT

The time slowed down once more this morning. It's every 14 days. It always takes 14 days... But with each time that it slows down, the fortnight only takes longer. At the very first second of every fortnight, we watch our clock in anticipation. It's a scientific clock, we would go insane without it. We watch hopefully as it shows each second take 0.25 seconds longer. Clearly, hope is not enough.
We are beginning to fall ill mysteriously, and we're struggling to grow our food under the artificial lighting... What will happen when time stops completely? We have absolutely no idea.

Markus Burrell (15)
Exhall Grange School, Ash Green

UNTITLED

In my dreams I travel back in time to millions of years ago when majestic dinosaurs roamed the Earth. Every night my dreams transport me to the gorgeous sight of dinosaurs. I stand transfixed at their magnificence. Who would have thought you could time travel in your head?
Absorbed in my dreams, I long to be living amongst these immense and fascinating reptiles. Without warning; my dreams become hazy. Is it my imaginary world glitching or is it me? Am I running out of time with my beloved dinosaurs?
I cling tenaciously to my dreams but they have regrettably vanished.

Tabitha Sayers (15)
Exhall Grange School, Ash Green

UNTITLED

I logged into my computer to complete an important task. There was something wrong; I just couldn't log in. I peered at the screen for ages. Without warning, a magnetic force sucked me into the screen. I struggled but the force was overwhelming. I stood in disbelief in what looked like a dark laboratory with networks and networks of wires. A voice bellowed from the chaos, "Hello, pleased to meet you at last! The name's Glitch."
At that moment, I knew I was inside my own computer.
"Sorry for disrupting your work but you looked like you needed a rest!"

Carys Homer (13)
Exhall Grange School, Ash Green

AGAIN

I walk into the town hall... There's the usual customer care desk and town attractions. But, there is something new, something odd, something different. Some sort of strangeness; an anomaly. Everyone else seems to ignore it, its sound crescendos, it beckons me. I go in.
A glitch, a strange buzzing noise reverberates violently. A noise so deafeningly loud that I feel my eardrums start to bleed, my sight goes dim. I wake up in some strange, altered version of Earth. It's a warm colour, it's like where I once knew. I wake up, I'm in the old, familiar town hall again.

Joshua Lumley (12)
Exhall Grange School, Ash Green

AN ENCOUNTER WITH A UNICORN

I opened the classroom door and there was a unicorn. It was biting its nails. As its nails fell to the floor, they turned into confetti.

It followed me to my English lesson.

It spoke to the teacher in the class and said, "Who's been good and who's been naughty?"

The teacher pointed to a pupil in the class called Bob and said, "He's been naughty."

The unicorn tilted his horn at Bob and made him disappear. Where Bob once sat a beautiful rainbow appeared, and the unicorn vanished into thin air.

Will I ever see it again? Hopefully.

Jamie Leigh (13)
Exhall Grange School, Ash Green

DISAPPEAR AND FADE

Life used to be simple, but now it isn't.

I spent days working for my family and in return, I achieved sleepless nights. On one occasion, I escaped from the house and into the bustling street. People exchanged rude glances and I felt like I didn't belong. People brushed past me without a care in the world and eventually, I felt lost. I found myself wandering into a space of darkness where people didn't thrive. I hid myself away for a while until a hand reached for me. The voice said, "Your time is now." I walked forth into the wilderness towards freedom.

Olivia Smart (16)
Exhall Grange School, Ash Green

A SHOW WITH A SMILE

A side of me still thinks it was fiction, yet it stood staring with a looming presence that day.
The past days I've been archiving some old episodes from a VHS, but something malicious was hidden within. The further I looked, another story was constructed, one of tragedy, revenge and hatred, with an entity ridiculed for what it became. All was revealed at the grand finale. The entity was alive, trapped for a few decades within this VHS, and it wasn't too happy when it finally escaped. I nearly died running away from it, and I'm frightened it'll strike again.

Peter Talbot (15)
Exhall Grange School, Ash Green

REFLECTION

I was brushing my teeth, like every night. I realised that my reflection wasn't moving with me. I stared deep into the ominous mirror. My reflection's eyes turned pitch-black. I froze in total shock and fear. From the mirror, a horrendous gurgling sound became more evident. While still frozen like ice, the thing in the mirror seemed to melt away. Its skin transformed into a humanoid creature with long nails and black rotten teeth. Without warning, the vision dissipated. Did I imagine this? Climbing into the safety of my bed, I closed my eyes. The gruesome image returned.

Cian Orme (14)
Exhall Grange School, Ash Green

THE SKY GLOWED RED

Early morning, and the sky glowed red. In the city, the esteemed marble statues of the city's founding rulers stood proud. Firstly, dear Sybil who was on the left, Rose on the right and proud Mary instilled in the middle.

However, there was an air of uneasiness. My bones softened, slowly disintegrating into the earth. My skin slid away like a fish out of water. I had sat too long, the fear at this moment was unbearable. I tried to think rationally and confront these monuments. I knew instinctively that their power prevailed always, even in death. They had won again.

Ethan Ames (15)
Exhall Grange School, Ash Green

A DEATH IN THE WORLD

I spotted something in the distance. It was a portal. It pointed far into space. I entered, petrified, and I met Death. "You're early, what happened down there?" said Death. I took my time, trembling words saying, "I don't know because there was a portal. Can I go back please?" Death glared at me and said, "Where is the portal?" I pointed at a wall where the portal had scorched itself a horrid shape. Death looked at me very confused. Had I changed my final destination? Would I ever get home? Would I ever see my family again? Help me...

Alicia Sullivan (14)
Exhall Grange School, Ash Green

RACE AGAINST DEATH

It went off. I could hear screaming and bombs behind me. I ran. I couldn't get captured again. That dreadful 'thing' was howling behind me. I had to do it. The howling was getting louder until the noise completely stopped. Everything was silent. I turned to see Death behind me.

He said, "The world has lived long enough."

I was still, my mind racing, but I could only say, "You can't have her, not again!"

Death got louder. Death was a child who had defeated me. A small child held the world in its hands. The child held power.

Ana McClean (13)
Exhall Grange School, Ash Green

THE GLITCH

She was on her way towards school, the time seemed as if it paused because the world around her had slowed down. Her schoolmates strutted past and were oblivious to her presence. The view in her peripheral vision was of rotted watercolour greys and black hues which posed as shrubs at her school. She paused in her footsteps while she gazed towards the power lines in the streets. Slowly they collapsed onto the ground in a loud thud. The girl's mouth was slightly agape with wonder. Utterly consumed with sadness, as she always was; she simply kept on walking nonchalantly.

Lexie Todd (15)
Exhall Grange School, Ash Green

CONTROL OF THE WORLD

He found the secret office, and he pressed it! The entire world was now under the hacker's control.

There was nothing I could do as I'd been directed out of the office. The hacker had sent us all to a fast food restaurant with a text to all employees. This would give him ample time to access the global system.

I wasn't going to let that happen. I dashed back to the secret office, the control centre of the world. Using my security clearance and programming skills, I reprogrammed the system.

The hacker's plan was foiled. The world was saved!

Charlie Hamilton (14)
Exhall Grange School, Ash Green

THE CLOCK WHICH STOPPED IN THE FUTURE

Vividly, I remember being in the hallway at school when every clock in every room stopped. I was terrified. At that moment I realised that I had been transported to the future. I didn't know what was happening. I was in a futuristic and fearless society where there were no limits, boundaries, or rules. Without warning, I found myself in the dark.

A person said, "You are safe! Come here to me now! It's me, come!"

I staggered around, stumbling and fumbling. A familiar hand stretched out and steadied me. It was my future self staring back at me.

Calum Wright (14)
Exhall Grange School, Ash Green

WHO?

I started regretting my decision of not leaving with him, due to the elevator glitch.

'Him' appeared and left before I could catch his name. I researched this figure and all I found was some conspiracy theorist. It was a dead end. I started to believe I was losing my mind. I mean I'm no one, just some burnt-out kid who's drifting through life filled with so little. Inevitably, my brain would imagine that I actually went on wild adventures and he was indeed an intergalactic hero. That was until without warning, he appeared and came back into my life.

Jake Greenway (17)
Exhall Grange School, Ash Green

MY LIFE IN PICTURES: THE GLASS MIRROR

It was a cold winter morning, frost clung to the window of my car. My job was to clear out the belongings of my late great-aunt. This house felt like no other I had ever been in before. Walking through this mysterious, forgotten house sent chills down my spine.

Something didn't feel right...

Pushing these feelings aside, slowly I made my way through the house, eventually reaching the final bedroom. Standing alone a huge object was covered with a white sheet.

Nervously, I tugged at the sheets. There it stood... The glass mirror. I saw my life in pictures.

Mimi Currie (17)
Exhall Grange School, Ash Green

IMMORTAL EARTH

Her eyes glazed over. Dead. The first death since the accident. How or why it happened is unknown. But she's dead.
I walked away from the table, unsure how to feel. I looked back once, still she lay there.
The accident was in 2031. The explosion. Everyone thought nothing of it until people stopped dying. The death count fell. Voices were louder. The riots got worse. The violence increased. Just for the sweet relief of death.
This girl changed it all. This girl had figured it out. She had done the impossible. She had achieved death.
Now it's my turn...

Madeline Standley (15)
Exhall Grange School, Ash Green

UNTITLED

Ignoring the warnings, I downloaded the app whilst I was in the air, on the plane. It appeared everyone had done the same. Without warning, the plane began to wobble and shake. Everyone started to scream and shout. Children were crying and clinging to their parents. Mums were trying to calm the children down, but they couldn't. The cabin crew couldn't help and they appeared to be frozen to the spot. To my horror, the plane descended lower and lower in the night sky. We knew instantly that we were now doomed.
If only I had listened to the warnings.

India Jackson (12)
Exhall Grange School, Ash Green

A GLITCH IN THE MATRIX

I didn't move, but my reflection did...
Am I dreaming? I rub my eyes in shock, nothing's changed.
I'm awake alright, this is no dream. Why did my reflection
move? Everything was perfectly normal last night when I
brushed my teeth in the mirror. What's so different now? I'm
sure I'm just seeing things, but what if I'm not? What if every
mirror is doing this to other people as well as me? Has there
been a glitch in the matrix? I don't know what to believe.
Am I even real anymore? My reflection fades away for the
last time.

Shaney-Ellis Fletcher (14)
Exhall Grange School, Ash Green

THE SUN

The sun always rose from the east, but one day it did not. Now in the Dragon Kingdom, it was dark. In the kingdom, there lived two dragons called Brightness and Shine, and Raya their daughter.

The dragon who stole the sun was an evil dragon called Darkness. The sun will never rise if he lives. When the dragons tried to stop him, he kidnapped them.

Thankfully, Raya got away. In Darkness' home, Brightness and Shine were in a cage. Without warning, Raya snuck in with a long spear and stabbed Darkness' heart.

That morning, the sun rose.

Eve Wood (11)
Exhall Grange School, Ash Green

DISTORTION

I dashed to the door to greet the delivery driver. It was the mirror for the bathroom. Armed with my drill, I carried the box up the stairs. I placed it on the floor; the box started moving by itself. *It's just my imagination playing tricks on me*, I thought. I drilled the holes in the wall, unwrapped the mirror and mounted it on the wall. Standing back to admire my work, frozen with terror, I was looking at myself. My reflection was different. I had bloodshot eyes, ripped clothes and open wounds. I didn't move, but my reflection did.

Joshua Powis (15)
Exhall Grange School, Ash Green

A SUDDEN CHANGE!

She buried her boy but he was back from the grave. His name was Harley. Tragically, he had been involved in a car accident and died instantly. It was a shock for his family who were broken by his death. Harley's mum had been driving and she had survived and had escaped with minor injuries.

She buried him with tears in her eyes. She placed flowers by the grave and blew him a kiss.

"Come back to life, Harly!" she wailed.

The next morning, she sat at the breakfast table. She turned around and heard Harley asking for toast for breakfast.

Bella Dowding (15)
Exhall Grange School, Ash Green

I THOUGHT HE WAS DEAD

Max woke up hearing gunfire and shouting. He quickly jumped up and grabbed his rifle. He could see everyone in the trench with him was dead. Curiously, it didn't look like they had been shot. He walked up the trench, quietly going past the dozens of dead bodies when he saw his commander lying dead... or so he thought. As Max peered over the top of the muddy trench, he could hear a groaning sound behind him. His commander's lifeless body was walking towards him. Overcome with fear and disbelief, Max raced towards his commander to help him.

Ashton Tomlinson (14)
Exhall Grange School, Ash Green

UNTITLED

Thinking back, what if we had never started this? What if it had never changed?

My thoughts started spinning as it was getting too much. I needed to snap back and rid myself of the thoughts I was buried in.

The world was near its end. No one or nothing was stopping the process now. Chaos was everywhere. This was it.

Global warming was going to take over us. Worry and panic were all anyone felt. What had we unleashed? It had overpowered us all in seconds.

It's all too much to endure! I can't take this. Goodbye, world.

Sophie Colley (13)
Exhall Grange School, Ash Green

STAND STILL

For a second everything stopped. Except for me, when I noticed for a second, the car next to me stopped dead before speeding away. Like an otherworldly entity had frozen the world except me. I didn't pay any attention to it until it happened again. I went into a local shop and picked something up, walked to the counter before time froze again but for longer this time. I seized on the opportunity and walked out then time resumed... How? How was I able to do that? That's when it dawned on me... I could control it and do whatever I wanted.

Joseph Williamson (17)
Exhall Grange School, Ash Green

THE TIME MACHINE

I finally did it! I created a way to freeze time. That machine, my life's work, complete!

I'd be able to write a journal or study. I could have been the smartest man, there would be no doubt about it. I readied the button, unlocked it, and was about to press it.

I took a deep breath of anticipation. *Click.*

The world around me went dark. I couldn't breathe. I couldn't move. I couldn't hear or speak. It was a nightmare, the world was ending, with the simple click of a button.

If only I had known.

Lucas Smith (14)
Exhall Grange School, Ash Green

I SAT IN THE LIVING ROOM WHEN THE BROADCAST CAME IN...

"We interrupt your programme to warn the public about the current threat in our nation..."
I didn't know what any of this meant or what they were going on about... Doppelgängers? While I wondered what this was all about, I heard my mother in the dining room call my name... "Ethan, Ethan, what are you doing down here with that weapon?"
Then I heard screams of terror and agony... then nothing but painful silence. It was unbearable... I heard myself come upstairs. Obliteration of the Doppel-Danger complete!

Reid Howarth (12)
Exhall Grange School, Ash Green

THE GAME

It was fantastic. One hundred points as I had completed a mission. Through my headset came an agonising screech. The TV opened up and a magnetic force sucked me into the screen. This was serious. I was an active participant in this game and other people could control my actions. Without warning, the lights flashed, and then suddenly Monster Man crept up on me. I screamed in horror. I ran for my life. There was no escape from the game. This was my new reality. A heart fell into my hands. My second life, so generously granted, but for how long?

Jack Hollis (12)
Exhall Grange School, Ash Green

THE MUSEUM

A group was walking through an abandoned office,
gathering items to show at a museum of office items.
However, a person in the group headed into a room and
saw a large golden bust. He decided to approach it and
ended up touching it.
Nothing happened so he went to find his group, but they
were not there. He searched all around but still did not find
his group.
But when he looked out one of the windows he was
surprised. The city surrounding the building was destroyed
and when looking at one of the computers, the date was
2423.

Elliott Clarke (13)
Exhall Grange School, Ash Green

I CAUGHT THE NUMBER 7 TRAIN BOUND FOR FRANCE

5:30pm, the train is stuck in a blizzard. The engines are not working. I'm on my phone now, I receive a text: 'Hey Calypso what's up?'
I ignore the message from Discord and climb into bed.
Clover and I keep texting about how I'm stuck in the blizzard in Switzerland.
Night comes and screams are heard. I lock myself in the toilets, screams intensify, sounds of violence and chaos.
There are footsteps... I open the door... It's Discord. Well, it's Discord's body but in her eyes, I see a vicious maniac.

Vanessa Wojcik (12)
Exhall Grange School, Ash Green

BE CAREFUL WHAT YOU WISH FOR

The battle was epic and we knew victory was ours. We were smashing the life force out of our enemies. I was chatting through the headset to Jago and he was rattling on about a new update and was bragging about his skill. He was laughing and boasting about how he really wanted to be inside the game. Suddenly, my headset crackled and hissed. At first, I thought Jago was mucking around until I looked back to the screen and saw Jago racing through a maze screaming for his life. He'd been sucked into the game and there was no escape.

Logan Madeley (12)
Exhall Grange School, Ash Green

WE BURIED IT... IT CAME BACK!

Patricia and Bob were a normal couple until a red object fell out of the sky and into their garden. Bob chucked it into the bin. Two weeks later, they woke up to a noise from the kitchen, but no one was there. They noticed the plants in their garden had gone red. One night, they woke up to discover a figure with a distorted, red, fleshy face. It was his dog, Lassie, who had unfortunately died years ago. How had he come back? On a rainy day, they had buried him. Unbelievably, Lassie had miraculously returned. Death is not eternal...

Alfie Southard (12)
Exhall Grange School, Ash Green

TIME HAS FROZEN

I woke up shivering, in a dark room. The sun had not risen. Utter silence permeated the atmosphere. Was I in an alternate universe?

Stepping outside, it was strange to see everything frozen. The cars had stopped, the birds were suspended in the sky and people stood like statues.

I stood in disbelief. For decades, the scientists had said that the environmental crisis was a ticking time bomb. Foolishly, no one believed it. Everyone thought it was hysteria until it happened.

Today was the day when nature finally won.

Saely Gurung (15)
Exhall Grange School, Ash Green

ROT

We should have never kept it here. I pleaded to them that it needed to be destroyed, cast away, forgotten. Yet they held it in their arms, fantasised about the wealth this artefact held. They were too far gone in its crimson stare. I had to get rid of them before they affected me and the artefact changed them. I can feel myself being eaten from the inside out, it crawls in my skin. I feel this golden creature call to me with its comforting whisper, through the stench of rot it consumes but it's never enough... It must feed.

Noah Alfie Patey (17)
Exhall Grange School, Ash Green

THE NIGHT THE WORLD FROZE

Every clock had stopped. The universal time system had been disintegrated. Every car on the street had slammed its brakes on. When I took a step forward, my reflection stood as still as a statue. When I called for help, my voice evaporated into the cold, windy air. There was not a sound in response, just the eerie echo of my voice in the wilderness. What imaginary world had I woken up inside? Was it all just a dream? I punched myself in the face. It hurt. This was real. Was I the only living creature left on this land?

George Revell
Exhall Grange School, Ash Green

THE GLITCH

The sun had not risen for five years, it had been pitch-black ever since it happened. Let me tell you how it happened five years ago.
In 1985, there was an astronaut who wanted to go to the moon. When he got to the moon, the engine malfunctioned and the rocket blasted into the sky, out of control. After a while, it crash-landed violently into the sun. Then the sun exploded. The astronaut was stranded on the moon for six months. Afterwards, he was saved but he was to blame for the sun exploding and the darkness.

Archie Parsons (13)
Exhall Grange School, Ash Green

WHERE AM I?

I lie on my hospital bed not being able to move or talk, trapped forever in my own mind. You see I always had a terminal illness, it's just not been that serious until a couple of years ago. Now, when I try to move like I used to, everything hurts. I've been put on life support and I've only got a couple minutes as I take my last breath. I ask myself why would God do this? Suddenly, everything goes black. I wake up enclosed in some pod. It looks futuristic and then a piercing white light blinds me.

Baydon Moffat (12)
Exhall Grange School, Ash Green

KILLER KITTEN

The small black box opened mysteriously. Inside was a kitten wearing a bow tie. I grabbed it and gave it a cuddle but little did I know that when it cuddled me it was spreading a deadly disease called Catvid 2023.

I panicked and called for someone. The only person who came was Jamie. She brought a bag and I threw the cat into the bag. But the cat had such sharp claws it ripped the bag and ran away out of sight. It was another mystery of the missing cat. It was waiting for his next victim to come along...

Ellsie Bagshaw (14)
Exhall Grange School, Ash Green

THE GLITCH

I lie in my desolate room. I am alone and I feel nothing but a sense of foreboding. I stare at the timer, hoping for it to glitch and speed up as I wait patiently for my death. My eyes are dark and heavy with envy. I'm envious of those whose timers have already stopped, envious of those who no longer have to be alone with nothing but their thoughts and the dreadful ticking of the timer. The ticking ricochets off my ear and I can no longer take it. I'm tired. I'm fed up. I want it all to stop.

Arlo Brown (15)
Exhall Grange School, Ash Green

MORTALITY HAS NO SYMPATHY

We buried him a fortnight ago. But he rose again. For two years, the country had been struck by plague! This was not the cause of John's fate. He was a flagellant. Every day he beat himself in the hope that God would spare him from this atrocious plague. In a way, this was successful. However, mortality seized him before he could be struck. We thought that once he was buried, it would be over. We were wrong. He returned, like dozens of others, serving plague until Armageddon called forth.

Oliver Lucking (14)
Exhall Grange School, Ash Green

CUTE BOX

I opened the door to a box. It was a heavy box that I had never seen before. It had a logo on it. *Toy Magic.* I thought it was some toy store order, as my wife had recently given birth. However, I asked my wife if she had ordered something for our child, and she said, "No." So I opened the box, and what I saw in there shocked me. It was a man - a decayed man! I called the police, and they shared with me that everyone had gotten a box. I'm still in shock to this day.

Annabel Soles (12)
Exhall Grange School, Ash Green

THE TIME MACHINE

As I get into the time machine, I change the time from 2023 to 1945. As I get nervous and contemplate everything, I press the button. I finally land, I walk out after feeling like I have been in a box for a day. Soldiers are standing and staring. As I look around, I see one, in particular, he looks at me, and I look at him. I find a gun in a dead soldier's hand. I pick it up and shoot him. I rush in the time machine, I change it back to 2023, just before they get to me.

Kitty Wearing (12)
Exhall Grange School, Ash Green

THE WOODS

We realise that we are lost. We encounter familiar voices and faces, ones we've met before on the outside. They are helpful and they claim to know the way back out. They urge us to halt and go no further. They tell us they've seen all there is to see. Leave while you can, they warn. They point to my jacket, ripped by a recoiling branch, and my exposed wound. We've come this far and what we left, we left for a reason, even if we can't recall it.

Harry Mair Tilley (13)
Exhall Grange School, Ash Green

THE RING

The ring that was supposed to keep the sun alive has just now failed. The sun is now expanding at a rapid rate and the Earth will be gone in a matter of days. We have no other option to save humanity but to load the transporters full of people and hope we land somewhere that is suitable for us. The transporters are now ready, and we have nowhere in particular to go. But we decide to go anyway. We did outrun the expanding sun, but now what? We will find out.

Oliver Poole (13)
Exhall Grange School, Ash Green

THE DAN SHOW

Dan was your average New Yorker, with a basic nine-to-five job, but not anymore. Time has stopped, but he hasn't, but other people have too, although the cameras haven't. They're following him, his every move. Suddenly, everything restarts. Dan foolishly thinks nothing of it. At work, he tells a dad joke to his coworker, but everyone laughs.

"This isn't serious, right?" Dan explains.

At home, he does some research and finds his wedding photo with his wife with her fingers crossed.

His life is a lie.

Benjamin Head (13)
Sandbach School, Sandbach

A PIECE OF THE SKY IS MISSING

A piece of the sky was missing.

I stared up at the black square that had replaced the sun and the clouds as people walked past unaware that the sun had disappeared.

I was the only one of many in this bustling city that was staring at it.

I bellowed, "Where is the sky!? It's missing!" but no one even batted an eyelid.

I glanced back at the black square. The square seemed to flicker back to the sun and the clouds were like a TV screen.

A piece of the sky was missing.

Brayden Fuller (14)
Sandbach School, Sandbach

THE GLITCH THAT WAS FOR THE WORTHY

All of a sudden, my clock stopped. Blue slime was splattered on my window to my left. I looked out to see slime falling from the sky. I reacted by grabbing my toy sword. Something was wrong. My sword was z-fighting with my wall.

Then I saw a grassy landscape. Ryu, my cousin, was there. We were frozen for two minutes. I started chopping trees. I felt a violent taste in the air. We started to chop trees.

It was only when I saw a bomb fall from a tree did I know. This was for the worthy.

Joseph Broad (13)
Sandbach School, Sandbach

IF WAR WENT THE OTHER WAY

Hitler won the war, and now the whole world is ruled by Germany. Every country is ruled by Hitler. Every man now has blonde hair, and blue eyes and is strong.

Several countries have joined the Axis, and a couple of years later there is a world lockdown because of a virus called Res-20. People have to stay at home to not catch it because it comes from sewage and releases bad gases.

During the lockdown, Hitler dies from it, and the world becomes allies and goes back to what it is now.

Adam Machnik (14)
Sandbach School, Sandbach

A NEW WORLD

Britain, 2023. The Nazi party took over after the war. It's not been the same since. Every man taken into captivity. The Ayrian race has taken over. Not just Britain. Not just Europe. But the world. All of us under new management. Alan Hitler, descendent of evil dictator Adolf Hitler. Everyone the same. Blue eyes and blonde hair. Almost as if they're all automatons. All acting, behaving and looking identical. The future of humanity destroyed.

Evan Davies (13)
Sandbach School, Sandbach

REFLECTIONS

I didn't move but my reflection did. Suddenly, my reflection jolted forward whilst I was brushing my teeth. I froze in shock, admiring what was in front of me. The reflection's hand grabbed me and pulled me through the glass mirror. I tried to scream for help, however it was already too late. My family was worried about where I was. I was confused, scared, worried. I'm sure people were going to miss me but how would I know? I'm still stuck.

Jacob Baker (13)
Sandbach School, Sandbach

THE CLOCKS BROKE

I was shopping in the mall with my friends. It was a normal day until every clock stopped. Everyone had frozen and all was silent. After hours of walking, trying to find some help, there was nobody. Then I strolled into a strange room. Out of nowhere, everything started moving again. I stood there thinking to myself, *what the hell just happened?*

Lucas Gibson (13)
Sandbach School, Sandbach

YOUNG WRITERS INFORMATION

We hope you have enjoyed reading this book – and that you will continue to in the coming years.

If you're the parent or family member of an enthusiastic poet or story writer, do visit our website **www.youngwriters.co.uk/subscribe** and sign up to receive news, competitions, writing challenges and tips, activities and much, much more! There's lots to keep budding writers motivated!

If you would like to order further copies of this book, or any of our other titles, then please give us a call or order via your online account.

Young Writers
Remus House
Coltsfoot Drive
Peterborough
PE2 9BF
(01733) 890066
info@youngwriters.co.uk

**Join in the conversation!
Tips, news, giveaways and much more!**

f YoungWritersUK **✗** YoungWritersCW

⊙ youngwriterscw **♪** youngwriterscw

**SCAN TO
WATCH THE
GLITCH VIDEO!**